transformation. Despite the span of its source material, it maintains an authentic, consistent voice pulled forward by its creative layout and line breaks. As a trans text, *listen—* moves towards self-acceptance beyond binaries without tidy answers and blurs the bias within sci-fi canon with confidence and care. It shined a warm light on the messy, poetic creature in me. I'm sure it will do the same for you." —Warren Longmire, author of *Bird/Diz: An Erased History of Bebop*

LISTEN—

A POETIC CREATURE

GRIFFIN ROCKWELL

LISTEN—A POETIC CREATURE

Edited by Holly Lyn Walrath.
Cover design by m. mick powell

Published by Interstellar Flight Press
Houston, Texas.
www.interstellarflightpress.com

ISBN (eBook): 978-1-953736-47-5
ISBN (Paperback): 978-1-953736-46-8

First Edition: 2025

Author's Note

This manuscript was originally submitted for my Master's in Science Fiction Studies from the University of Dundee. (As a poet, when given the choice, I obviously took the creative dissertation option!) In the work, I wanted to acknowledge the rich history and canon of science fiction—starting with the genre-sparking work of Mary Shelley's *Frankenstein*—while still creating a new creative work that would be both original and express my own interests and concerns.

In the dissertation, I gave myself a triple challenge. First, I wanted the manuscript to be one long poem, something I had never done before. For my second challenge, I decided to follow in Frankenstein's footsteps and make this manuscript one long cento: a poem composed of lines from other texts. Historically, this has only been done using lines from other poems. However, I complicated the challenge by taking the words and lines from science fiction novels rather than poems. This resulted in my final challenge: turning prose lines into poetry through line and shape on the page. Ultimately, I feel I've created a cohesive voice and narrative in this manuscript, which is no small feat given that I was working with twenty-one authors and twenty-six texts.

I find the cento interesting for several reasons. First, it is an inherently intertextual conversation, as lines are juxtaposed next to each other without context. This allows a variety of texts to interact, and, in fact, this project was interesting because most of these science fiction works had not conversed before I brought them together, coming as they were from different eras and authors. Also, I enjoyed the requirements of the cento to cite sources and so acknowledge those who have shaped the work; I always enjoy learning about what works and authors have shaped my favorite author's works, as it gives me an understanding of what they have loved (and of course, more things to read!).

The cento is part of a tradition of "found poetry," created by selectively erasing words and sentences from a source text to leave behind a new poem. Blackout and erasure poetry are some of the most common ways to encounter found poetry, such as in Mary Ruefle's *A Little White Shadow* (2006) or Chase Berggrun's *RED* (2018). Many times, this erasure can be powerful and a means of reclaiming power (such as in *RED*, where a trans woman author examines womanhood and power using *Dracula* as its source text, a book that often strips agency from its female characters). Erasure poetry can be a way to "take back" words and power from documents or texts that do not give it to the subject(s) of said texts.

However, authors like Solmaz Sharif have noted that found poetry is not only political but can be inherently violent as someone else's words are literally being effaced to form something new (originally noted in an essay from *The Volta*, "The Near Transitive Properties of the Political and Poetical: Erasure," Issue 28, April 2013). The cento would at first appear to be the opposite of effacement, as the original authors' words are being preserved, merely reworked into new contexts to give them alternate or surprising interpretations—

a means of dialoguing with other poets and the poetic canon (or in this case, science fiction authors and canon). However, the cento is just as violent as erasure—merely in a different way.

Rather than erasing another writer's words, in a cento, the source text is, to use a Frankenstenian allusion, dismembered and dissected for parts according to whatever the surgeon finds most valuable or useful. For better or worse, I chose to become Frankenstein in this project as much as possible, embracing the role and taking from various sources to furnish my "poetic Creature"— my unified body made from parts and pieces. This approach allowed me to make even the cento's form and style an experiment with the Frankensteinian mindset. This was directly tied to the idea of wanting to create a work that was wholly my own creation, even if pieced together from other work.

However, it was critical to me—a trans, agender author—to find a voice in the cento that *was* wholly my own. This was particularly important as the voices I was drawing from were strongly gendered, and masculine voices were disproportionately represented. Of my twenty-six sources, only six were written by women; additionally, though two feature gender-bending narrators, less than half feature feminine protagonists as narrators—and only three feature women as sole narrators.[1] However, in the breaking of line, use of space, and

---

[1] The two featuring genderbending protagonists: Le Guin's *The Left Hand of Darkness* and Delany's *Stars in My Pocket Like Grains of Sand*; the nine featuring women narrators: Beukes' *Moxyland*, Butler's *Kindred*, Delany's *Babel-17*, Dick's *The Man in the High Castle*, Herbert's *Dune*, Liu's *The Three-Body Problem*, Okorafor's *Binti*, Robinson's *Red Mars*, and Russ's *The Female Man*; the three featuring women as sole narrators: Butler's *Kindred*, Okorafor's *Binti*, and Russ's *The Female Man*.

exploration of themes of silence and self-discovery, I introduced a non-traditional, nonbinary element that pushed the cento towards a more "neutral" voice and style.

In isolating "I" statements and fragments and divorcing them from their original context, I was able to strip away much of what tied the characters to gender. For example, Axel from *Journey to the Centre of the Earth* and the Traveller from *The Time Machine* are emphatically nineteenth-century men (which is reflected in their perspectives in the original texts), but their statements, when isolated, do not convey this. This was a personal and political choice in creating the cento and was crucial to making the work have a unified voice and narrative I could claim. By the time I finished the cento, its words and phrases hardly felt like they belonged to others. Here, I have made something mine and not-mine: The words are emphatically not mine, yet the cento is mine in voice and vision.

A few final, formal notes: I have replaced any instance of the word "and" with a "+" to mimic the visual of stitches (also done in the suture-like section breaks) and to reflect the Frankensteinian themes of the cento's stitched-together "Creature." Additionally, all the punctuation and italicization are as represented in the original text; I have not added to or changed the text as originally quoted apart from replacing the word "and" where it occurs. While the spelling fluctuates between American and British variants, all quotes are as presented in the original texts. A complete list of in-text references and a list of sources for the cento can be found in the endnotes.

Thank you to every author for what they have given me (and the world) in publishing these works, and thank *you* for reading what I've made of them.

listen—
a poetic creature

Hear my tale; it is long
+ strange
                    I warn you
that what you're starting

to read   is full
of loose   ends
+ unanswered questions.

          It will not be neatly tied up
          at the end, everything

resolved + satisfactorily explained

all this will be absolutely incredible

to you. To me the one incredible thing is
that I am here   I've tried

to close my eyes to it, but
I'm not going to any more

   What I ask of you is reasonable
   + moderate   You must not

          breathe a word   of this

               to anyone

I must say
what I must say. It is
already decided

                              I must be bold now

All this happened,
          more or less
Now, listen to me

- / - / - / - / - / -

I have, doubtless,
excited your curiosity

Shall I make my report?

                              *Let's fucking get it
                              over with, already*

I'll make my report
          as if I told a story
I'm going to write a poem,
          I think. But
it may be a novel. I have
          a lot to say

I entreat you
to hear me

- / - / - / - / - / -

A quotation had started
the train of thought

          It is good to have an end
          to journey towards; but
          it is the journey
          that matters, in the end.

I allowed myself to be

governed by   the impulses

          of the moment

scattered   like the debris
of some   nameless meteor

mind,   apparently,   was dwelling
on strange things   the Thing

that was to bring so much

          struggle + calamity—such a
          small thing. Yet, it contained

                    a mystery . . .   A blank +
                    intricate absence   in all
                    its immense potential:
                    tabula rasa, blank slate

It was a vast thing, beyond

knowing, a sea

of information coded
in spiral + pheromone, infinite

          intricacy that only the body,

                    in its strong blind way,

                              could ever read

- / - / - / - / - / -

That glimpse,
like all dread glimpses of

truth, flashed out   from an

          accidental piecing   together

                    of separated   things

two seemingly un   connected
strands, now

          twisted together, made the world un

familiar overnight

A process cannot be understood

          by stopping it. Understanding

                    must move
                              with the flow
                                        of the process,

                              must join it
                    + flow with it

I was thinking   now,
+ in the faint starlight
I carefully picked out
the broken   fragments
one by one

          I had   an intuition—

it's all about putting together many

     apparently un   connected

          things. When you piece them together

        the right way,

     you get the truth

So   I must break through
all reticences   at last—even about

that ultimate
     nameless
        thing

There will be difficulties,
     discrepancies,
        but I must at least supply
the basic structure

     I feel sick at the thought

of how much has to be done,
how much time it's all going to take,

      the hundreds + hundreds
      of interconnections   I am

about to proceed on a long
+ difficult voyage   But

      deep down inside me,
      I wanted . . . I *needed* it.

I couldn't help but act on it
to see the Thing more clearly

- / - / - / - / - / -

Everything began spinning away
into blackness   I saw around me   nothing
but a dense + frightful darkness   Darkness
fell in from every side, a sphere
of singing black, pressure on
the   extended   crystal nerves
I stared out at the darkness fighting
to calm myself   In the dark something
fell   I leaned against the window + tried
not to look outside into the blackness
Lost, so small amid that dark
I listened, straining in the darkness
for some reply—a shout, a sigh.
I heard nothing   lost in darkness eternal,
I was (at least for the moment) nowhere at all!

    compressed at the heart of all that dark,
    there came a point where the dark could be
    no *more*,   + something   tore
    The darkness   seemed to grow

                         luminous

   Starlight displaced   just enough
   of the night to charge each shadow

with menace

     all I could think of to do

was wait   until dark

+ it was suddenly
        dark again,
the ordinary night sky standing overhead
as if nothing had happened   a black + comfort

less sky   The blackness is emptiness - vast
emptiness stretching out infinitely   But it's only
in the utter black that you can feel the true scale,
the volume + weight of that gaping unknowable
its inky nothingness   lost in darkness
+ distance   solemn with the sudden realisation
I located the unorganized body
+ I realise this is the end of something.
Maybe not limbo so much as

                          the falling space

- / - / - / - / - / -

       every experience
       before this night,

                had become
               sand cur
                 ling
               in an
              hourglass

Before, dark + opaque bodies
had surrounded me, impervious

to my touch +
sight   glittering
with thousands
of watching eyes

       I knew my silence
       disquieted them

I told as much of the truth
        as I could   the mouth

is left empty, a lost   referent

You're not bored by my talking
all this time? Ah, good. Well,
to make sense of what happened
later, I have to tell you all this.

The world was to me
a secret, which I desired

to discover   to ask questions
I had to struggle to understand

   It was a queer, neck-ruffling thing,
   a faintest suggestion   I could feel it

   in my finger tips, an actual physical sensation,
   a compelling urgency to do something,

+ I sat there, my fists clenching
+ unclenching

I've fought nicely against
it as long as I could . . .

The cracks grew fast
My thoughts were far away . . .

why are you unhappy?

                    I'm not unhappy.

- / - / - / - / - / -

        I would wake up   full

of rage, a feeble shaky rage

       that turned into feeble tears
       I do not know how far my
       experience
       is common   I craved to be like
       everybody else   gradually felt
       more

      + more

         alienated

             from the world

Already, my body felt as if
it were no longer mine; I'd let it

                       go

In fact everything   about me
has become unnatural; I've become
an unnatural   self   I confess

that I could not put on a brave face

I felt cut off + cowered
inside my own mind   I felt as if

I had committed
         some great crime

- / - / - / - / - / -

Anyway,

my life passed day after day
accompanied by this strange feeling,

+ before I knew it   The idea

    of departure   was suddenly

        more real

Of what a strange nature is

knowledge!   It clings to the mind

is burned into my recollection
because of its crucial position

in my life. It marked my   loss

      I lost about a year of my life
      + much of the comfort
      + security I had not valued
            until it was gone

A thought,

    at first vague + ill defined,

resolved itself in my mind
into a certainty   The mere presence

of the idea was an irresistible proof

    of the fact

I knew that something strange
had happened, + for the moment

could not distinguish what the strange thing

might be   For this kind of thing,

     you have to
     think outside
          the box

This, I thought,
was the moment
          of decision

     You need to learn

     to face   the abyss!

- / - / - / - / - / -

to wonder about
the unknown realm

               beyond

I asked
what I most wanted

    to know

I can almost
     feel it, I know
if only I could turn

around in the right direction,
     I'd be able to reach

out my hand   + take it

      I resolved to take steps   toward

investigation   But it must be

      done with utmost secrecy

I didn't know what else to do—
or even whether there was anything

I could do   Maybe

the answer lay in the past,

      in some obscure crevice
      of memory   I went back

      to the beginning, to the first
      dizziness, + remembered it all

Simplicity had departed;
the dream had faded

into disturbing   complexity

Time + identity—

      the two great mysteries . . .

I was at first
unable to solve these questions; but

   perpetual attention,   + time,
   explained to me

many appearances which were at first

enigmatic

At once, I felt both part of something

historic

      + very alone

- / - / - / - / - / -

Alone, with appalling

      abruptness,

solitude was my only

consolation—deep, dark,
death-like solitude

    Filled with so many emotions at once,

    it was impossible   not to be

    confused   I feel fractal with
    nerves   I flung myself into

      futurity. At first

        I scarce thought of stopping,
         scarce thought of anything

    but these new sensations. But presently

    a fresh series of impressions grew up
in my mind—a certain curiosity + therewith

a certain dread—

reflected, refracted, + magnified
by such layers   Curiosity made

a small, unfriendly fist

        Perhaps

                        I should not hope to convey
                        in mere words the unutterable

guided by dread
+ the lack of dread

I was exhausted
with the violence of my

        emotion

- / - / - / - / - / -

I avoided
explanation, + maintained

a continual silence

I didn't know the words,

        the grammar,

                the syntax

        Or is it

        that I'm not facing the situation?

I am without a face . . .

I am not seen. I speak +
        am not heard. I come +
        am not welcome   I
        am   a mask, concealing

the real. Behind me, hidden,
actuality goes on, safe

from prying eyes   I don't know

        why, though. I can't
        see - yes, I do

The body was

meat
all golden, all benign
dun-colored, blurry, its details hard to make out
the taste of old iron, scent of melon, wings of a
moth
an anxiety that almost amounted to agony
like a star, always so distant
a shark thing, gleaming like obsidian,
the black mirrors of its   little island of daylight
all new, all strange: it was absolutely impossible
to compare it to anything
considered a question mark

    I have no power
    of explaining it

it was the *general outline*
of the whole which made it
most shockingly frightful

my body + soul were

         exactly the same

What was the difference?

I don't know

      anything about it   I could not
      face the mystery   the abyss

remained all around
+ this Thing I saw!

How can I describe it?

- / - / - / - / - / -

The tremendous significance lies
in what we dared not tell—

what I would not tell now
but for the need   But no,

      not quite, there was still

         something, something to be

heard   +   spoken . . .

Listen:
      Something cannot emerge
      from nothing   I now felt
      as if a film had been taken
      from before my eyes

Soon I will know

Urged on   by an impulse
which I cannot definitely analyse
I took the risk because I think

        the time has come to take it

                I want to know why

I cannot describe to you
my sensations on the near prospect
of my undertaking. It is impossible

        to communicate to you a conception
        of the trembling sensation, half
        pleasurable + half fearful,

with which I am   preparing
to depart.
                I am going
                        to unexplored regions

        I was inspired   by the spirit

of discovery   but in silence,

        always   in silence

- / - / - / - / - / -

left alone, un

        acquainted with the language
        of the   silence   welling in

lonely, desolate, so long

that it was intolerable.

      You could follow it
      + go forward or backward
      as long as you liked, but

you'd never find   the end

I knew about loneliness
the loneliness comes from

      the question   a bold question,
      + one which has ever been considered

        as a mystery

The question, a vacuum
where no information would come
to answer who or what or why,

made an   emptiness   I attempted

to speak, but the words
      died away

voices were   divorced

    from bodies   a silence

greater than the silence of the desert

descended

    Oh,
      the dead

              silence!

- / - / - / - / - / -

        Silence is not

     what I should choose, yet

it suits me better than a lie

the solitude,
          the desolation,

had been endurable
        but   all to no purpose

I don't know
what you suspect,
but it has happened

      the open
         ing,

           the   widening,

the mind forced to sudden

     growth   Nothing is so painful

to the human mind as a great
+ sudden change   there was

     a persistent, pervasive
     hint of stupendous secrecy
            + potential revelation

all sense of balance   gone

It's easy to be

       led to the abyss

- / - / - / - / - / -

the full   temerity
of my voyage came suddenly

upon me   it was not meant
that we should voyage

       far

I began to get panicky.
       Time was passing. I wasn't
    finding what I was certain was here

somewhere,
   + what I had to find

     if it wasn't already too late

I shut up, as well as I could,
in my own heart

     the anxiety that preyed there

I cut + hardened then,
I think   I had been all in

   pieces, dis
    integrated

my heart yearned
to be known   + loved

I am a crumpling façade

The universe is full

of doors   all opened

upon me at once

the nightmarelike feeling
caught up   Worry, doubt,
+ fear were twisting
through my mind   I felt
a wave of emotion that was
 near akin to tears

I cannot back down.
I must hold control

the expectation took
the colour of my fears

*I must not fear. Fear is the mind-
killer. Fear is the little-death
that brings total obliteration.
I will face my fear. I will
permit it to pass over me
+ through me. + when it has
gone past I will turn
the inner eye to see its path.*

Where the fear has gone
there will be nothing.
Only I will remain.

I was glad

when the mirage began

to break up

I have my cat,
I have my room,
I have my hot plate
+ my window
+ the ailanthus tree

Things are always
        going to be
falling apart
                So it goes

I was undisturbed
by thoughts   finally
found myself adrift + free

Beware; for I am

fearless, + therefore

                powerful

- / - / - / - / - / -

But how

was I to direct
myself?   My first thought

was to discover   The answer

to that question   to examine
the thing   silhouetted
against the sun

like a Stuka   or a pterodactyl
alien + haunting   one end
connected to the endless past,

          the other to the endless future,

+ in the middle only the ups + downs

Beautiful, or harsher than that:

spare, austere,
stripped down,
silent, stoic, rocky,
changeless. Sublime

visible +,

in its own way,
alive

- / - / - / - / - / -

suddenly   I saw it

          the whole truth

rushed into my mind

I knew a thousand things

it would take minutes to explain,
+ others I can never explain

        in a lifetime

It is real,
the real thing,

the thing behind
        the words

It's a mirror   +

there's something

        inside   infinity,

mirror into mirror

           Labyrinthine

complexity   Something

with no framework

        or credulity   curious,

specific
+ resonant   private
+ sheltered from all eyes,
+ right now

        I was grateful for that

in this a micro-universe,

complete

how wide it was,

how deep it was,

how much was mine

                    to keep

I was unable   to contain

myself

- / - / - / - / - / -

WHAT WAS THAT?

- / - / - / - / - / -

Something rips free inside me

- / - / - / - / - / -

I wept, without precisely understanding it

- / - / - / - / - / -

Why then did I not

        speak out?

There was a
        queer,
        flat,
        dead silence

                          I shall not fear . . .

there was no   honest
explanation I could give them—none

they would believe   I'm in
something I don't understand

        I wasn't born into it. I came to it. I chose it
        I'm under compulsion myself. + I don't know

            why   I mean to discover the secret of this
            I'd like to understand, so I won't hurt

      + just like that, I understood

                      We have to name ourselves first.
                      + you don't know who you are

To my shame, I realized
I was almost crying. I needed

        desperately

to be   alone

        I was

+ there was no way out.

I shut my eyes tightly
as the tears came. I curled

my body + stayed like that
for several minutes

The quiet
          was profound

- / - / - / - / - / -

I slackened my progress.
I could hardly sustain

the multitude   of feelings

          I come to a place
          where it is very
          difficult to proceed

The *effort*
it had taken
          to ask that question

It was very hard work

          my sense of loss deepened
          + my sense of shock grew

                    What an ordeal
                    it was going to be

you should know
by now, I can talk
my way out of
          anything

yet I am lost   I could not remember
how I had meant to weave the story

What can I say?

                                        Why am I doing it?

- / - / - / - / - / -

Weary.
So it goes

my storms
of emotion

have a trick of
          exhausting   themselves

I had done enough talking
+ learning
+ hoping
          to be transported home

I can't say
I really know
exactly what happened,
          or why,
          or just how it began,
                    how it ended;

                    or if it has ended

The stability was

illusory   the clarity of mind

retreated   like a loss of confidence
The whole business   is complicated

          past endurance

                    How much I have

                    to learn

- / - / - / - / - / -

Ignorant as I knew I was,
I trusted   myself

it did not seem mis   placed
Once you start   it's too late

to back off
          I settled into a
more usual routine—usual
          for someone like me
          in a situation like mine
          on my particular world.
          In my particular place on it.

Only now
I'd had a year to see how
unusual, in universal terms,
my usual could be   —it was

an entirely new experience

the colour of television, tuned to a dead channel

rising like the waves of a troubled sea

Loud + noisy at the beginning, calming to this at the end

The unpleasant sensations
of the start   were less poignant now.
They merged   at last   into

a kind of hysterical   exhilaration
the ineffable majesty of the

            whole

    its electrical   radiance

        Its answers - they're

        queer, somehow

- / - / - / - / - / -

I was, it seemed,

            a key   I am

            invented

            gone hollow. That was it:

                                    I'm a seed

Now I could never

go back   The way

your brain works it's always rewiring
itself   an entire body of knowledge

driven into   Mystery

of body organism,
its own knowledge

—outwardly   normal

　　I'm the abnormal one now. Normalcy
　　　was a majority concept, the standard of many

did not this star-fashioned image
prove it?   define itself
at the center of things   put

　　　a stamp of strangeness on me

- / - / - / - / - / -

At first
　　　　I started back, unable
　　　　to believe that it was indeed
　　　　I who was reflected in the mirror

I felt hopeless
　　　　　　　ly cut off
　　　　　　　from my own kind—   struck

with the notion of something

so large   it might as well be

　　　　infinite

how could it help but be political?

Do you believe that I am
what I say I am?   I know

        I'm human. I can't prove it

Neither man nor woman,
neither + both

expression became   enigmatic
It . . . seemed the right way

It's going to be getting into
everything   an infinite

        blue space

It's   my storm

- / - / - / - / - / -

The lost   breath returned
+ an unfamiliar thing

was happening   The most
important thing   I learned

I am complex

        enough,

in my narrow ways

What I've been doing is

        to go along with the exterior motions

because it is safer   But now

I am awake + alert   I have to
make a place for myself here. That means

work   Changing

it won't de

stroy it. Reading its

past might get harder,

but the beauty of it won't

go   away

Emphasise importance
of   discovery

But there's nothing more
I can really say about it,
other than that it's   Lonely . . .

I   wanted to be there   immediately,

no careful years of waiting
What I've seen
is enough, + I don't need any more

confirmation   No one can conceive

the variety of feelings   which bore me
onwards, like   a hurricane   Every morning

I had to believe it all over again

I tried to brace up
for the worse rigours

      to come

I'm not sure   I'm ready

- / - / - / - / - / -

What I mean is   I can't

answer right away.
      You'll have to accept that   I
don't have to. I don't have to make my motives

transparent   before I speak of it to you

      again

I have written myself
into good spirits   It was

the only thing I knew
to do. I—   I feel

with only too much keenness
the inadequacy of pen + ink—

      proof   of the otherness

I did not qualify my   Words,
+ their easy patterning

      The words were outlined
      in brilliance. There was

            an edge to them

I resolved not to fail

in my purpose

- / - / - / - / - / -

I felt

                                        the silence

I could talk + describe

            endlessly; but

        that was all

I had to give

                Finally,

just as the frustration became
almost   intolerable,

its departure or defeat
was a relief or a release

The end is near

                It is all brand new

It was possible to tell   a point

I think we should all hear

I was   impatient . . .

                                        I wanted

         to get out

What world will you give me?

What world will I have?

A new light
seemed to dawn

              upon my mind   Carefully,
              with a plodding precision

I'm going to try to do

something, + I don't know

              if I can or not

I will send a message

voice the cry of a bird
unknown

- / - / - / - / - / -

I told him

                    who I was

- / - / - / - / - / -

Listen—

I talked a lot

I wondered whether or not
he believed me, but

it didn't really matter   For we can never

go back. We must go forward. We must
find   our own way

The experience did make me
a little more confident   I understand

some of it

        better than I did

I've gone a long way

I had worked hard
for nearly two years

I know it now

        I'm sorry I waited
            so long

I was named,
        known,
        recognized;

I existed.

It was an intense relief

I was now   free

Everything was beautiful,
+ nothing hurt   I don't even remember

 the last time I had to go to the aquarium
+ stifle my sobs by watching the sharks

                    I could get used to this

People aren't supposed to
look back. I'm certainly not going to do it

        anymore

I did   what I couldn't do

this opened before me
a wide field for wonder + delight

+ now I have things to say
that are all my own

- / - / - / - / - / -

I had an obscure feeling
that all was not over

        Who am I? What am I?

That was one of those questions
 that was fated always to remain

            unanswered   I found myself

dwelling on that dawn absence   But

            I can feel myself tiring of all this

Nothing remained to say

            rain + the sound of trains

            a body grown in upon itself

    I know, I know

Talk of something else,

something

            that will bring

                        peace

ENDNOTES

CENTO REFERENCES (BY SECTION)

[*opening*] – p.1

Shelley 79 | Finney 1 | Wells *TM* 118 | Asimov 14 |
Shelley 122 | Verne 34 | Moorcock 107 | Herbert 397
| Vonnegut 1 | Finney 13

-/ - / - / - / - / -

[*make my report*] – p.2

Shelley 13 | Dick *Androids* 74 | Liu 55 | Le Guin 1 |
Delany *Babel* 192 | Shelley 78

-/ - / - / - / - / -

[*a quotation*] – p.2

Matheson 104 | Le Guin 220 | Shelley 130 | Verne 84
| Lovecraft "Cthulhu" 385 | Wells *WW* 7 | Herbert 44
| Delany *Stars* 11 | Robinson 108 | Gibson 265

-/ - / - / - / - / -

[*piecing together*] – p.3

Lovecraft "Cthulhu" 382 | Liu 192 | Herbert 34 |
Finney 54 | Dick *Androids* 96 | Liu 144 | Lovecraft
"Mountains" 805 | Moorcock 106 | Beukes 254 |
Shelley 5 | Okorafor 29 | Wells *WW* 11

-/ - / - / - / - / -

[*darkness*] – p.6

Matheson 152 | Shelley 158 | Gibson 284 | Butler 14
| Delany Stars 84 | Okorafor 51 | Gibson 35 | Verne

139 | Delany *Stars* 103 | Gibson 284 | Wells *TM* 99 |
Herbert 220 | Finney 175 | Robinson 442 | Shelley 40
| Asimov 55 | Beukes 74 | Wells *WW* 88 | Shelley
196 | Herbert 39 | Asimov 31 | Beukes 196

-/ - / - / - / - / -

[initial disquiet] – p.7
Herbert 201 | Shelley 80 | Le Guin 4 | Shelley 36 |
Butler 3 | Delany *Babel* 42 | Liu 205 | Shelley 19-20 |
Butler 1 | Campbell 1 | Finney 183 | quoted in
Vonnegut 15 | Liu 240 | Herbert 62 | Russ 119

-/ - / - / - / - / -

[full of rage] – p.8

Le Guin 286 | Wells *WW* 30 | Le Guin 8 | Liu 294 |
Okorafor 37 | Dick *Androids* 182 | Verne 110 | Le
Guin 65 | Shelley 138

-/ - / - / - / - / -

[knowledge] – p.9

Liu 191 | Herbert 35 | Shelley 98 | Lovecraft
"Mountains" 798 | Butler 1 | Verne 218 | Shelley 56 |
Wells *TM* 122 | Liu 364 | Shelley 111 | Verne 46 |

-/ - / - / - / - / -

[steps towards investigation] – p.11

Lovecraft "Mountains" 808 | Le Guin 61 | Russ 145 |
Lovecraft "Mountains" 798 | Dick High Castle 63 |
Butler 216 | Matheson 39 | Butler 9 | Matheson 115 |
Moorcock 57 | Shelley 88–89 | Okorafor 80

-/ - / - / - / - / -

[*alone*] – p.13

Dick *Androids* 106 | Shelley 69 | Robinson 45 | Beukes 166 | Wells *TM* 25 | Lovecraft "Mountains" 865 | Delany *Babel* 97 | Lovecraft "Dagon" 26 | Vonnegut 52 | Wells *WW* 29

-/ - / - / - / - / -

[*the body*] – p.14

Shelley 160 | Delany *Babel* 19 | Dick *High Castle* 73 | Le Guin 22 | Dick *High Castle* 227 | Asimov 35 | Gibson 6 | Le Guin 106 | Liu 101 | Gibson 244 | Shelley 38 | Liu 69 | Gibson 200 | Wells *WW* 117 | Robinson 171 | Dick *High Castle* 95 | Shelley 63 | Lovecraft "Cthulhu" 383 | Russ 5 | Matheson 54 | Vonnegut 4 | Wells *TM* 69 | Herbert 330 | Wells *WW* 44

-/ - / - / - / - / -

[*I want to know why*] – p.16

Lovecraft "Mountains" 801 | Delany *Babel* 126 | Vonnegut 16 | Herbert 222 | Shelley 146 | Herbert 187 | Lovecraft "Dagon" 27 | Le Guin 140 | Dick *High Castle* 88 | Shelley 8 | Verne 207 | Le Guin 170

-/ - / - / - / - / -

[*silence*] – p.17

Shelley 104 | Delany *Stars* 15 | Liu 295 | Butler 288 | Delany *Stars* 365 | Shelley 32 | Delany *Babel* 62 | Shelley 192 | Robinson 251 | Verne 153 | Russ 77

-/ - / - / - / - / -

[*widening*] – p.19

Le Guin 273 | Wells *WW* 172 | Lovecraft
"Mountains" 798 | Asimov 235 | Delany *Babel* 96 |
Shelley 172 | Lovecraft "Mountains" 799 | Dick *High
Castle* 225 | Liu 74

-/ - / - / - / - / -

[*fear*] – p.20

Wells *TM* 27 | Lovecraft "Cthulhu" 381 | Finney 55 |
Shelley 166 | Campbell 28 | Le Guin 289 | Shelley 109
| Beukes 286 | Herbert 512 | Shelley 34 | Liu 160 |
Finney 88 | Wells *WW* 175 | Herbert 437 | Wells *TM*
79 | Herbert 9 | Lovecraft "Mountains" 800 | Russ 3
| Robinson 330 | Vonnegut 23 | Shelley 51 |
Lovecraft "Dagon" 25 | Shelley 144

-/ - / - / - / - / -

[*examine the thing*] – p.22

Shelley 116 | Shelley 57 | Herbert 102 | Campbell 9 |
Robinson 246 | Gibson 223 | Liu 295 | Robinson 121
| Dick Androids 15

-/ - / - / - / - / -

[*suddenly I saw it*] – p.23

Lovecraft "Dagon" 28 | Shelley 170 | Finney 223 | Le
Guin 166 | Liu 406 | Wells *WW* 13 | Gibson 98 |
Lovecraft "Mountains" 821 | Matheson 17 | Delany
Stars 71 | Finney 148 | Dick *Androids* 146 | Vonnegut
13-14 | Shelley 42

-/ - / - / - / - / -

Delany *Stars* 352

-/ - / - / - / - / -

Beukes 292

-/ - / - / - / - / -

Shelley 105

-/ - / - / - / - / -

[*realisation*] – p.27

Verne 24 | Asimov 210 | Herbert 259 | Butler 1 |
Dick High Castle 200 | Le Guin 182 | Gibson 227 |
Verne 14 | Delany *Babel* 120 | Okorafor 55 | Delany
Babel 161 | Butler 239 | Okorafor 33 | Asimov 5

-/ - / - / - / - / -

[*ordeal*] – p.28

Shelley 54 | Lovecraft "Mountains" 853 | Herbert 45 |
Russ 153 | Finney 121 | Dick *High Castle* 77 | Delany
Babel 192 | Shelley 183 | Le Guin 182 | Delany *Stars*
128 | Herbert 236

-/ - / - / - / - / -

[*weary*] – p.29

Vonnegut 25 | Wells *WW* 49 | Butler 26 | Finney 1 |
Liu 75 | Okorafor 33 | Asimov 77 | Dick *High Castle*
108

-/ - / - / - / - / -

[*the new*] – p.30

Butler 161 | Campbell 2 | Dick *Androids* 186 | Delany
Stars 108 | Robinson 15 | Gibson 3 | Shelley 76 |

Delany Babel 47 | Wells *TM* 24 | Lovecraft
"Mountains" 787 | Verne 150 | Asimov 168

-/ - / - / - / - / -

[*I'm a seed*] – p.31

Le Guin 119 | Delany *Babel* 96 | Robinson 124 |
Herbert 214 | Okorafor 66 | Beukes 65 | Gibson 130
| Dick *High Castle* 231 | Vonnegut 127 | Matheson
159 | Lovecraft "Cthulhu" 394 | Gibson 270 |
Herbert 27

-/ - / - / - / - / -

[*human*] – p.32

Shelley 91 | Wells *TM* 48 | Delaney *Stars* 446 |
Robinson 79 | Le Guin 33 | Campbell 48 | Le Guin
214 | Dick *Androids* 126 | Herbert 119 | Robinson 131
| Gibson 72 | Herbert 489

-/ - / - / - / - / -

[*work*] – p.33

Delany *Babel* 50 | Vonnegut 19 | Gibson 285 | Dick
High Castle 115 | Liu 10 | Butler 82 | Robinson 213 |
Lovecraft "Mountains" 790 | Delany *Stars* 277 |
Moorcock 45 | Robinson 485 | Liu 135 | Shelley 35 |
Le Guin 242 | Lovecraft "Mountains" 779 | Russ 87

-/ - / - / - / - / -

[*words*] – p.35

Moorcock 46 | Dick *High Castle* 243 | Beukes 175 |
Delany *Babel* 105 | Shelley 47 | Matheson 138 | Wells
TM 20–21 | Robinson 122 | Le Guin 117 | Delany
Babel 62 | Herbert 12 | Shelley 179

-/ - / - / - / - / -

[*speaking*] – p.36

Shelley 143 | Le Guin 247 | Liu 90 | Delany *Stars* 14 | Lovecraft "Dagon" 29 | Vonnegut 103 | Dick *High Castle* 91 | Campbell 9 | Le Guin 50 | Delany *Stars* 222 | Delany *Stars* 222 | Shelley 21 | Matheson 68 | Delany *Babel* 20 | Moorcock 118 | Gibson 289

-/ - / - / - / - / -

Vonnegut 3

-/ - / - / - / - / -

[*I know it now*] – p.38

Vonnegut 57 | Le Guin 98 | Butler 227 | Robinson 273 | Butler 190 | Delany *Babel* 19 | Dick *High Castle* 56 | Shelley 38 | Herbert 60 | Delany *Stars* 263 | Le Guin 111 | Shelley 70 | Vonnegut 88 | Russ 29–30 | Beukes 7 | Vonnegut 16 | Dick *Androids* 175 | Shelley 96 | Delany Babel 16

-/ - / - / - / - / -

[*all was not over*] – p.39

Shelley 70–71 | Moorcock 57 | Robinson 389 | Delany *Stars* 437 | Herbert 408 | Dick *Androids* 48 | Gibson 284 | Gibson 190 | Delany *Stars* 94 | Shelley 67

Cento Sources

Asimov, Isaac. *I, Robot.* HarperVoyager, 2018. First published 1950.

Beukes, Lauren. *Moxyland.* Penguin, 2018. First published 2008.

Butler, Octavia. *Kindred.* Headline Publishing Group, 2018. First published 1979.

Campbell, John W., "Who Goes There?" in *Who Goes There?* Gollancz, 2011, 1–75. First published 1938.

Delany, Samuel R. *Babel-17.* Gollancz, 2010. First published 1966.

———, *Stars in My Pocket Like Grains of Sand.* HarperVoyager, 2019. First published 1984.

Dick, Philip K. *Do Androids Dream of Electric Sheep?* Gollancz, 2010. First published 1968.

———, *The Man in the High Castle.* Penguin, 1965. First Published 1962.

Finney, Jack, *The Body Snatchers.* Gollancz, 2010. First published 1955.

Gibson, William, *Neuromancer.* Gollancz, 2016). First published 1984.

Herbert, Frank, *Dune.* Hodder & Stoughton, 2005. First Published 1965.

Le Guin, Ursula K., The Left Hand of Darkness. Gollancz, 2017. First published 1969.

Liu, Cixin, *The Three-Body Problem.* Translated by Ken Liu. Head of Zeus Ltd, 2015. First published 2008.

Lovecraft, H.P., "Dagon," in *The Complete Fiction of H.P. Lovecraft*. Quarto Publishing Group, 2014, 25–29. First published 1919.

———, "The Call of Cthulhu," in *The Complete Fiction of H.P. Lovecraft*. Quarto Publishing Group, 2014, 381–407. First published 1928.

———, "At the Mountains of Madness," in *The Complete Fiction of H.P. Lovecraft*. Quarto Publishing Group, 2014, 776–865. First published 1936.

Matheson, Richard. *I Am Legend*. Gollancz, 2010. First published 1954.

Moorcock, Michael. *Behold the Man*. Gollancz, 1999. First published 1969.

Okorafor, Nnedi. *Binti*. Tor.com, 2015.

Robinson, Kim Stanley. *Red Mars*. HarperVoyager, 2009. First published 1992.

Russ, Joanna. *The Female Man*. Gollancz, 2010. First published 1975.

Shelley, Mary. *Frankenstein; or The Modern Prometheus*. Gollancz, 2012. First published 1818.

Verne, Jules. *Journey to the Centre of the Earth*. Penguin, 2009. First published 1864.

Vonnegut, Kurt. *Slaughterhouse-Five, or The Children's Crusade: A Duty-Dance with Death*. Vintage, 1991. First published 1969.

Wells, H.G. *The Time Machine*. Gollancz, 2017. First published 1895.

———. *The War of the Worlds*. Gollancz, 2017. First published 1898.

Griffin Rockwell is a queer poet who can frequently be found writing about gender, science, space, and unusual connections. Xe is the author of the Elgin Award-nominated chapbooks *body in motion* (*perhappened press*) and *Lexicon of Future Selves* (*VA Press*), as well as two microchapbooks; their work has appeared in *AGNI, Cotton Xenomorph, Whale Road Review, Palette Poetry*, and elsewhere. Find xer website and socials at https://linktr.ee/griffinrockwell.

m. mick powell is a queer Black Cape Verdean femme, an artist, an Aries, and author of the chapbook *threesome in the last Toyota Celica* (*Host Publications*, 2023) and *DEAD GIRL CAMEO* (*One World Books*, 2025).

www.mickpowellpoet.com

Acknowledgments

I have so many people to thank for bringing this project to life, and although I know I won't be able to name everyone (and may inadvertently leave someone out), I want to thank a few people specifically for their help.

Firstly, to Keith and Heather: I so appreciate your help with shaping this manuscript into a strong Master's dissertation for the University of Dundee. You helped me challenge myself, and I am so grateful for your time and insight throughout the process! I so enjoyed working with you during the initial "galvanization" of this poetic Creature.

Thank you to the friends who helped me push through the dissertation process, whether it was in general encouragement or in reading and commenting, but especially (in alphabetical order): Anzal, Damiana, Gwen, Laura, Lucy, and V. Thank you also to my family, who supported me throughout the Master's program and beyond. Your enthusiasm for the project (and my success) means the world!

To Holly: Thanks for being willing to give this a read when I pitched it despite it being out of the regular submission period and for your belief in and support of this book. I am so grateful that this manuscript has been in your thoughtful and careful care and I appreciate everything you've done for it and me! I'll be eternally thankful to IFP for publishing this poem that's near and dear to my heart.

To mick: your cover is beautiful and astounding! Thank you for being willing to give me such an incredible piece of art to go with the poem and for your work in creating it. Your art takes my breath away every time I look at it, and I remain so grateful for your friendship, support, and talent!

I also want to thank every author (and translator) whose words formed this cento. Science fiction has always inspired and fascinated me, and these authors and their worlds have helped me open my mind and envision new possibilities. Even if they'll never know it, I am grateful to them for their works, even as I borrowed and Frankenstein-ed pieces of their text into something of my own. Their words quite literally gave me mine.

And last (but certainly not least), I want to acknowledge you, Reader. Your willingness to go on this journey with me is something I don't take for granted. Thank you for your support of me and my work! I am deeply grateful.